The way
i love
you

David Bedford & Ann James

LITTLE HARE

I love…

the way we
play our
games,

the way you run so fast,

the way you
come straight
back.

That's the way I love you.

I love…

the way we
always share,

the way you're
my best friend,

the way we
both pretend.

That's the way I love you.

I love…

the way you tell me things,

the way you
jump so high,

the way you
smile your
smile.

That's the way I love you.

I love…

the way you understand,

the way you show me how,

the way we are
right now.

That's the way I love you.

I love…

the way you always care,

the way you're always there,

that's the way I love you.

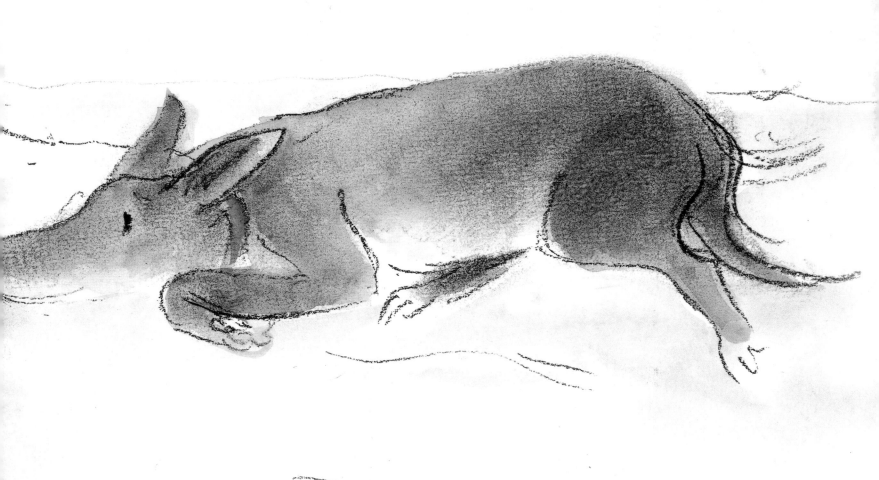

That's the way I love you.